Eating Enchiladas

Simply Sarah

Eating Enchiladas

by Phyllis Reynolds Naylor

illustrated by Marcy Ramsey

Marshall Cavendish Children

First Marshall Cavendish paperback edition, 2011

Marshall Cavendish Corporation
99 White Plains Road, Tarrytown, NY 10591
www.marshallcavendish.us/kids

Library of Congress Cataloging-in-Publication Data
Naylor, Phyllis Reynolds.
Eating enchiladas / by Phyllis Reynolds Naylor; illustrated by Marcy Ramsey. — 1st ed.
p. cm. — (Simply Sarah)
Summary: A sleepover inspires Sarah, who likes to do things differently, to chose Mexico for her "Countries of the World" presentation.
ISBN 978-0-761-4-5300-0 (hardcover) 978-0-7614-5885-2 (paperback)
[1. Geography—Fiction. 2. Mexico—Fiction. 3. Mexican Americans—Fiction. 4. Individuality—Fiction. 5. Schools—Fiction.] I. Ramsey, Marcy Dunn, ill.
II. Title. III. Series.
PZ7.N24Eat 2008
[Fic]—dc22
2007028356

Book design by Vera Soki
Editor: Margery Cuyler

The illustrations are rendered in ink and wash.

Printed in China (E)
A Marshall Cavendish Chapter Book
1 3 5 6 4 2

For Ava Quinn and Alexa Josephine,
with love
—P. R. N.

To Rosie, my little enchilada
—M. R.

Contents

One	Great, Great, Great, Great	1
Two	Grandfathers	10
Three	Being a Queen	17
Four	Sleepover	24
Five	Eating Enchiladas	33
Six	Talking in the Dark	39
Seven	Sarah's Choice	47
Eight	Yams and Legs and Chopsticks	57
Nine	Mercedes' Day	64

* * *

One

Great, Great, Great, Great

Sarah Simpson wanted to be anything but ordinary.

Her name was ordinary, but she couldn't do anything about that. Her face and hair were ordinary. She couldn't change those, either.

She lived in an ordinary apartment building on an ordinary street in Chicago. But every chance she got, Sarah Simpson tried to be different. She liked to think of ideas that no one else had thought of.

Sometimes she wore a blue lace in one sneaker and a green lace in the other. At school she put ketchup on her carrots instead of her fries.

On the playground, she wore her jacket over her head instead of her shoulders. And at night, when she read to her little brother, Riley, she made up her own story to go with the pictures as she turned the pages of the book.

"The Idea Girl!" her father called her. But some of her ideas were better than others.

One day Sarah's teacher, Mrs. Gold, had something to tell the class.

"We're going to be learning about different countries," she said. "We're going to find out how people in other places live."

Sarah thought she would like this. It would be more fun than adding numbers and spelling words.

"We'll learn what people in other countries eat," said Mrs. Gold. "We'll learn what games they play and what kind of clothes they wear."

"What country will we learn about first?"

asked Peter, Sarah's friend.

"Well, each of you will choose a country," the teacher answered. "I want you to learn all about it and share what you learn with the class. Perhaps the country will be someplace you have visited. Maybe it will be the place where your ancestors were born."

Sarah knew that ancestors were relatives. Relatives who lived long ago.

There was a large map of the world at the front of the room. Mrs. Gold named some countries. She showed where they were on the map.

"You can learn about a country by checking a book out of the library. You can look it up on the Internet. Perhaps you could watch a program about the country on TV," said Mrs. Gold. "Or you could talk with people who have lived there."

Sarah and Peter walked home together after school. Peter Grant lived in the apartment below Sarah's with his grandmother. Sarah lived on the top floor,

the fourth, with her mother and her brother, Riley. Sarah's father worked overseas building bridges.

The Simpsons' apartment was called a loft. Bookcases and screens divided up the space instead of walls. A skylight in the ceiling let in lots of light.

"What country are you going to choose?" Sarah asked as they walked along the sidewalk.

"Nigeria," Peter told her. "That's in Africa."

"Why did you choose Nigeria?" Sarah wanted to know.

"Because my great-great-great-great-grandfather came from Nigeria," said Peter.

Sometimes Peter talked a little silly, Sarah thought. She had a grandfather in Maine who was really great, but she did not go around saying that he was great, great, great, great!

When they got to the apartment building, they went up to the third floor to tell Granny Belle that Peter was going to Sarah's, as usual, for cocoa.

"I'll be at Sarah's," Peter called from the doorway. He stooped down to pet his cat, Patches.

"All right," answered Granny Belle. "But you come back in an hour."

Sarah and Peter climbed the stairs to the loft. Sarah's mother was getting the cups ready on the table. Most days after school, Sarah's friends came up for cocoa.

Sarah had just taken off her jacket when there was a knock at the door. Mercedes Mendez and her cousin Leon came in. They lived in the building next door. They didn't go to Sarah's school. A yellow bus came around for them each morning and brought them back in the afternoon.

"The Cocoa Club!" called Riley when everyone was there. He liked to sit at the table with the other children and listen to them talk about what had happened that day. Riley made up stories of his own.

This time he said, "I got a cut on my finger."

"That's too bad," said Mercedes.

"I almost cut my finger off," Riley went on.

Sarah looked at his finger. "Riley, that's only a little cut," she said.

"*Uh-uh!*" said Riley. He held his finger up in the air. He kept it bent so it looked as though half of it were missing. "It fell into my soup," Riley said.

Leon, who was younger than Mercedes, almost believed him. He stared.

"It fell into my soup, and I ate it," said Riley.

"Riley!" Mom scolded. Riley only laughed. Then the others laughed, too, even Leon.

"Today in school we talked about countries," Sarah said. "Peter's grandfather came from Nigeria."

"My great-great-great-*great*-grandfather," said Peter.

There he goes again, being silly, Sarah thought.

"Well, today I waited for a phone call from New York, but it never came," said Mom. "Now I'll have to wait until tomorrow to find out if my pictures were any good."

Sarah's mother was an artist. She painted pictures for books for an art director in New York.

"Today I lost an earring," said Mercedes sadly. Mercedes had tiny holes in her ears for earrings. She said that her mother had the holes made when she was just a baby.

"What earring did you lose?" Sarah asked.

"A silver one that looked like a bell," said Mercedes.

Sarah was sorry to hear that. The bell earrings were her favorites. They made little tinkling sounds when Mercedes moved her head. Mercedes got them from Mexico.

"Today I found a penny," said Leon. "You can have it if you want, Mercedes."

He reached into his pocket. He pulled out a baseball card. He pulled out an eraser, a marble, some string, a bottle cap, and the penny.

"No, thank you," said Mercedes. "You can keep it, Leon."

It was not the same as the earring, Sarah knew. Anything that came from Mexico was special to her friend. Sometimes it seemed to Sarah that while Mercedes lived here in Chicago, her heart was back in Mexico.

Two

Grandfathers

When everyone had gone home, Sarah kept Riley busy while Mom worked on another picture. Sarah's job was to play with her little brother for an hour each day after school so that Mom could finish her work and get dinner started. Sarah earned fifty cents an hour.

"What do you want to do today, Riley?" Sarah asked.

"I don't know. *You're* taking care of *me*!" Riley said.

"We could pretend we live in Africa," Sarah told him.

"Or we could pretend we don't have any fingers," said Riley.

He bent all the fingers on his right hand so that it looked as though half his fingers were gone. Then he bent all the fingers on his other hand.

Riley tried to pick up a ball with all his fingers bent. He tried to pick up a cup of water and spilled it on the floor.

"*Please*, Sarah!" came Mom's voice from across the loft. "You're supposed to be entertaining Riley."

Sarah got out the blocks and started to build a castle.

At dinner that night, Sarah asked, "Where was I born?"

"In a hospital," Mom told her.

"I mean *where*?"

"In Maine. Up where Grandpa lives."

"In the United States?" said Sarah.

"Of course."

"Oh," said Sarah thoughtfully. After a while she asked, "Where were *you* born, Mom?"

"In Illinois," said her mother.

"Where was Dad born?"

"New Jersey, I think."

"Weren't any of us born in a different country?" asked Sarah. "How can I choose a different country to talk about if we were all born here?"

"Sorry, Sarah. We were all born in the United States," her mother said.

Sarah did not want to stand up in front of her class and talk about the United States. That was so ordinary. The children in Mrs. Gold's class already knew about the United States. They *lived* in the United States. She wanted to choose a country that was different.

"I know!" Sarah said suddenly. "I could choose the country where Dad is and ask him about it when he calls on Sunday."

"That's an idea," said Mom. "But he's worked in several countries."

"Then I'll talk about the one he liked best," Sarah told her. "Peter is going to tell us about Nigeria because his grandfather came from there. Peter doesn't just call him great. Peter calls him great-great-great-great-grandfather."

Mom laughed. "Peter's talking about his grandfather's father's father's father's father, that's why," she said.

Sarah put down her roll. This was hard to understand.

Mom tried to explain. "Your grandfather's father is your great-grandfather. *His* father is your great-great-grandfather. *His* father is your great-great-great-grandfather, and *his* father is your . . ."

"Great-great-great-great-grandfather," finished Sarah.

"Right," said Mom.

Riley thought about that, too. "Do *I* have a great-great-great-great-great-great-great-great . . ."

"Yes," said Mom. "You can say the word *great* as long as you like, and you still have that kind of grandfather."

Sarah felt dizzy just thinking about it. "Did *all* of my great-grandfathers come from New Jersey?"

"Of course not. Long ago, your grandfathers came from just about everywhere."

"But what *countries*?" Sarah asked.

"I'm not sure, honey. Russia, Poland,

and England, I think."

Sarah did not know very much about Russia or Poland. *England!* Maybe she could stand up in front of the class and tell everyone about England.

Riley had finished eating and was trying to walk around the floor on his knees, holding his feet up behind him.

"Riley, what on earth are you doing?" Mom asked.

"I'm trying to walk without any feet," said Riley.

"Why?" asked Sarah.

"Because I got a cut on my leg today. I almost cut my leg off!"

"Oh, Riley! You and your stories!" said Mom.

Three

Being a Queen

At school the next day, Emily Watson told Sarah that she was going to tell the class about Italy. She was going to find out as much as she could, because her mother had been born there.

Sarah didn't know much about Italy.

Tim Wong said he was going to tell about China. Sarah knew a little about China, but she had never been there.

"Have we ever been to Italy?" she asked

her mother that night as she took a bubble bath and Mom helped wash her hair.

"No. I'd like to go there, but we have never been," her mother told her.

"Have we ever been to Nigeria?"

"Nope," said Mom.

"Where *have* we been?"

"We've been to Maine and Vermont and New Jersey. I went to California once, but that was before you were born."

"At school I have to talk about a country," Sarah told her. "Maybe I'll talk about England."

"That would be nice," said Mom.

There were bubbles everywhere. Bubbles in the bathtub. Bubbles on the floor.

Sarah piled the soapy bubbles high on her head.

Mom laughed. "You look like Martha Washington," she said.

"Who's that?" asked Sarah.

"The wife of our first president," Mom told her.

There was just too much to learn before she was grown-up, Sarah thought as she dried off and put on her pajamas. She had to learn about countries. She had to learn about presidents. She would have to know how to get a job. She would have to know how to cook a chicken and drive a car.

Riley came into the bathroom to brush his teeth. Sarah was still thinking about countries.

"Tell me everything you know about England, Mom," she said.

"That would take all night," said her mother. "What do you want to know?"

"What do the people in England look like?"

"Just like us, Sarah."

"What do they wear?" Sarah asked.

"The same kind of clothes," said Mom.

"What do they eat?"

"The same things we do. And a lot of kidney pies, I think," Mom said.

That sounded pretty awful to Sarah.

"What do they do for fun?" she asked.

"Honey, the English are very much like we are. They speak the same language and wear the same clothes and play games and go to parties, same as you."

"But isn't there *anything* different about England?" Sarah asked. Maybe she wouldn't choose England after all.

Mom thought for a minute. "Well, there's Buckingham Palace, where the queen lives."

A queen!

Sarah could go to school dressed as a queen. She could wear a crown on her head and a long dress. She could stand in front of the class in her long dress and her crown and tell everyone about England.

"Do we have a long dress I could wear to school?" she asked.

"I think we could fix one up for you," said Mom.

"Could we make a crown? I want to be a queen," Sarah said excitedly.

"My goodness!" said Mom. "If you're

going to be the Queen of England, we will certainly make you a crown."

"Can I be a queen, too?" asked Riley. "I want a crown."

Sarah laughed, but Mom said, "I suppose, Riley. A king, anyway."

When Sarah came home from school the next day, a wonderful surprise was waiting. Mom had taken an old curtain and turned it into a beautiful gown for Sarah. There was a ruffle around the neck. There was satin beneath the skirt, and the gown reached all the way down to the tops of Sarah's feet.

Sarah gasped when she saw it. This was no ordinary dress. This was a gown for a queen!

But that wasn't all. There on the table was a golden cardboard crown. It had sparkles. It had pearls. And when Sarah set it on her head, she didn't even look like the same girl who walked to school each

morning with Peter. She looked like a queen who should be riding in a coach pulled by two white horses.

"It's so beautiful!" Sarah said, hugging her mother. "I'll be the most extraordinary person in class. And I'll tell them all about Buckingham Palace and the queen."

"Then I hope you'll read a few more books, Sarah," said Mom, "because there's a lot to say about England."

Four

Sleepover

Sarah did read a book about England, but she read a lot more about the queen. She learned all about Buckingham Palace and the Changing of the Guard.

When her father called on Sunday, as he did every week, Sarah waited until it was her turn to talk. Then she said, "Guess what I'm going to be at school next week."

"A dragon? A wizard? Whatever it is, it'll be special, I know," said her dad.

"It's something about a country," Sarah hinted. "Guess which one."

"Brazil?" Dad guessed.

"No," said Sarah.

"Germany? France? Japan?"

"No, no, and no," said Sarah.

"England?" said her father.

"Right!" cried Sarah. "And I'm going to be the queen."

"Wow!" said her dad. "Have a good time, Your Majesty."

Each day when Sarah got home from school, she tried on the dress and the crown. She decided she would wear her good summer shoes with the dress, even though her toes stuck out. She would put polish on her toenails.

All she could think about was how special she would feel walking the four blocks to school, looking like a queen.

But another nice thing happened, too. Mercedes invited Sarah to sleep over at her place on Friday.

Sarah was very excited. She had never slept at anyone's house before, except her

grandfather's up in Maine.

"May I go, Mom?" she asked.

"I think so, but be sure you have clean pajamas."

"Could I wear my dress and crown?"

"That's not a good idea," said Mom. "Mercedes invited *you*, not the queen."

Sarah could hardly wait until Friday. Mom got out a small bag for her to use.

On Wednesday, Sarah put clean pajamas in the bag.

On Thursday, she put in some clean socks and underpants.

On Friday, she packed her toothbrush.

"I'm invited for dinner, too," she said.

"You're a very lucky girl," said Mom.

At school on Friday, Sarah kept watching the clock. She wanted it to be three o'clock so that she could go to the sleepover.

"Next week you'll begin sharing what you've learned about other countries," said Mrs. Gold. "Who's ready to talk about a country?"

Emily Watson raised her hand.

Peter Grant raised his hand.

Tim Wong raised his hand. So did some of the others.

"Perhaps you could bring things from that country, if you have them, to show to the class," said their teacher.

Sarah smiled to herself. She needed to read a little bit more about England, but just wait until the teacher saw *her* walk in with her dress and crown!

At last the bell rang. Sarah ran out the door.

"Why are you in such a hurry?" asked Peter.

"I'm going to a sleepover at Mercedes's," said Sarah. "Have you ever been to a sleepover?"

"No," said Peter. "I've never been to a sleep*under*, either." And he laughed.

Peter makes weird jokes sometimes, Sarah thought.

There would be no Cocoa Club that afternoon because Sarah was going next door.

"Good night, Riley," she said to her brother.

"Are you going to bed already?" Riley asked.

"No, but you won't see me until tomorrow," said Sarah.

"Have a good time," said her mother.

Sarah put on her jacket and picked up her bag. She went downstairs to the lobby.

Mr. Gurdy was there. He took care of the building. He was washing the windows.

"Good night, Mr. Gurdy," said Sarah. "I'm going on a sleepover."

Mr. Gurdy didn't even look up. "Sleep tight. Don't let the bedbugs bite," he said.

Sarah walked up the sidewalk and into the building next door. She climbed up the stairs to the second floor. She climbed up the stairs to the third, then to the fourth. She knocked on the door of the Mendez's apartment. Mercedes lived with her cousin Leon and his mom and dad and baby brother.

Mr. Mendez came to the door. He was Leon's father and Mercedes's uncle.

He had a mustache that curled at each end. His hair was shiny black. He smiled at Sarah.

"Is that Sarah?" called Mrs. Mendez from the kitchen.

"I'm here for the sleepover," Sarah said.

"Oh, no! Not another girl in this house!" said Mr. Mendez. He pretended to close the door in Sarah's face.

Mercedes ran in from the other room. She was laughing. "Yes, another girl in this house!" she said. "Come on in, Sarah."

Leon was watching TV. The baby was sleeping.

Mercedes took Sarah to her room. It was tiny with a narrow bed and a sleeping bag on the floor.

"You can have the bed," said Mercedes.

It was a pretty room. The bed had a blanket with bright red and yellow flowers on it. There was lace around the blanket. The curtains at the window were lacy. There was a big poster on one wall of blue and yellow parrots.

The whole room looked like another country. Sarah smiled. Tonight she would be sleeping in Mexico.

Five

Eating Enchiladas

"Do you want to help us make dinner?" Mercedes asked.

"Yes!" said Sarah.

Sarah followed her friend into the kitchen. Mrs. Mendez was wearing an apron over her red dress. The apron had lace. Everything in the Mendez apartment seemed to have lace.

"What are you making?" Sarah asked.

"We're having enchiladas," said Mercedes's aunt. "Do you like them?"

"I don't know," Sarah told her.

"Do you like chili?" asked Mercedes.

"Yes," said Sarah.

"Do you like pizza?"

"Yes," said Sarah.

"Then you will like enchiladas," Mercedes said. "First we start with tortillas."

Mrs. Mendez was placing flat circles on a platter. They looked like big, thin potato chips.

"Now," Mrs. Mendez said to Mercedes, "put some of these chopped olives on top of each tortilla."

She handed Sarah a saucer full of cheese. "And your job will be to sprinkle cheese on top of the olives."

"It all smells very good," said Sarah.

Three tortillas with cheese and olives were placed on top of each other. Mrs. Mendez made another stack, and another. On top of each stack, she placed a fried egg. On top of the fried egg, she poured some spicy tomato sauce.

Leon came to the door of the kitchen.

"I'm hungry," he said. "What are we having for dinner?"

"Enchiladas with eggs," Mercedes told him.

Soon the whole apartment was filled with the wonderful smell of tomato sauce with onions and pepper. The meal was ready, and steam covered the kitchen window.

Everyone sat down. There was a special place for Sarah at the table.

"Waaaaah!" came a cry from one of the bedrooms.

"Oh, dear," said Mrs. Mendez. "I hoped Luis would sleep a little longer."

"I'll get him," said Mercedes. She went into the bedroom and came out with the baby. She put him in his high chair.

Luis looked at Sarah and smiled. Sarah smiled back.

"Have some enchiladas, Sarah," said Mr. Mendez, passing the platter.

Sarah helped herself. She would go home the next day and tell Riley that she had eaten enchiladas with eggs.

It was different being in Mercedes's apartment. It wasn't better than it was at home. It wasn't worse than it was at home. It was just different.

Mr. Mendez did not help in the kitchen. He didn't help with the dishes. When Leon left chocolate marks on the sofa, his mother didn't punish him. She sent him to his father to be scolded.

When Mr. and Mrs. Mendez talked to each other, they didn't speak English. They spoke a language Sarah did not understand.

"Are they speaking Mexican?" she asked Mercedes.

"No, they're speaking Spanish," Mercedes said.

Sarah thought that people who spoke Spanish lived in Spain. She didn't know that people spoke Spanish in Mexico.

She asked if she could help with the dishes.

"Do you know how you could help the most?" Mrs. Mendez said. "You could help by playing with the baby while Mercedes and I do the dishes."

So while Mr. Mendez read to Leon and Mercedes helped with the dishes, Sarah played with Luis. She got out his toy caterpillar and ran it along the floor. She played peekaboo. She played patty-cake with the baby's feet.

When Luis began to smell bad, she went to the kitchen and said to Mercedes, "I'll change him if you show me how."

"I'll help," Mercedes said.

It was very gross, but Sarah did it.

When the baby had been changed and

fed and put into his crib again, Sarah and Mercedes and Leon played Pick Up Sticks at the table. Finally it was time for bed.

Sarah took a bath. Mercedes took a bath. They brushed their teeth together and said good night to Mercedes' aunt and uncle.

Then Mercedes crawled into her sleeping bag and Sarah got into bed. Sarah was only in the building next door to her own, but it seemed as if she were in a different country.

Six

Talking in the Dark

"Do you like living here?" Sarah asked Mercedes as she stared up into the darkness.

"Most of the time," Mercedes said.

"Have you always lived with your uncle and aunt?" Sarah wanted to know.

"Since Mamá and Papá died," said Mercedes.

Sarah didn't know that Mercedes had lost her parents. "What happened to them?" she asked.

"They were killed in an earthquake," said Mercedes. "They were on vacation. They were in a hotel. I was at home with my grandmother."

The room was very quiet.

"That's when Uncle Carlos sent for me. He said I could live with them in the United States. So I came."

"That's so terrible!" said Sarah.

"I know," said Mercedes. "But you know what I like best about living here in the city?"

"What?" asked Sarah.

"The Cocoa Club," Mercedes told her. "And having you next door."

"I'm glad," said Sarah.

"You know what I like worst?" Mercedes asked.

"What?" said Sarah.

"That they won't let us speak Spanish at my school. They want us to learn to speak good English. And I can't wear whatever I want. We have to wear uniforms."

Sarah thought about how lucky she was to wear whatever clothes she wanted to school. In fact, *she* was about to go to school dressed like the Queen of England! But maybe this wasn't the best time to tell Mercedes that.

Through the open window came the sounds of night in the city—the same sounds that Sarah heard from her window at home. There were whistles and horns. There were sirens and people laughing. The clock was striking in the tower.

Sarah knew that back in her family's loft, Riley and Mom were listening to the same sounds. They were all hearing the same noises, but here, somehow, it seemed different.

And suddenly Sarah knew what country she wanted to talk about in Mrs. Gold's class. Maybe she did not want to put on a long dress and crown and be the queen after all. She did not want to say that the people of England ate the same food and wore the same clothes and spoke the same language as people in the United States.

She wanted to tell her class about this night in the apartment with Mercedes—about enchiladas with eggs. About the blanket with the red and yellow flowers on it and the poster of parrots on the wall. She wanted to say that the people in Mexico spoke Spanish, and that sometimes there were earthquakes. She would choose Mexico for her country.

The next morning, Sarah was the first one awake. She opened her eyes and looked up at the ceiling. She did not see the green plant that hung above her bed back in the loft. She did not see the picture her mother had painted of deer in a forest.

She saw a mobile of little paper donkeys going around and around above her head. She saw lace curtains at the window and Mexican lady dolls in long dresses on a shelf. She saw a little dancing man and a little woman made out of tin beside a row of books.

And she saw Mercedes in the sleeping bag on the floor with only her nose sticking out.

Ting, tong, ting! came the sound of wind chimes outside the window.

Sarah wondered how it felt to be

Mercedes, coming to a strange land to live in a new apartment with her uncle and aunt.

"*Buenos días,*" somebody said. Mercedes was awake now and looking at her.

"What?" Sarah asked.

"That's 'good morning' in Spanish," Mercedes said.

So Sarah said "*Buenos días*" right back. Then she said, "Guess what?"

"What?" asked Mercedes.

"I'm choosing Mexico for my country."

"What do you mean?"

"In school," said Sarah, "we each have to choose a country to talk about. We have to bring in things to show from that country. I'm going to choose Mexico because I like your apartment."

Mercedes rolled over and sat up. "What will you say about Mexico?" she asked.

"Whatever you tell me," said Sarah.

Mercedes giggled. "Say that the houses are made out of chocolate," she said.

Now Sarah began to laugh.

"Say that the rivers are cocoa. Say that the trees are made of candy."

They both laughed.

A smacking, snapping, scratching sound came from the doorway, and Leon came in. He was pretending to be an alligator. He crawled around over Mercedes's sleeping bag.

Mercedes scrambled up onto the bed. She and Sarah jumped up and down, and Leon tried to catch them when they tumbled off.

Tap, tap, tap.

Mercedes and Sarah stopped jumping. The tapping seemed to be coming from under the floor.

Mercedes put her finger to her lips.

"It's the woman downstairs," she said. "She always taps on her ceiling with a broom handle if we make too much noise."

Mrs. Mendez came to the door of the bedroom. She was wearing her robe.

"Mercedes, you girls aren't making too much noise in here, are you?" she asked.

"We'll be quiet," said Mercedes.

Leon hid under the bed and pretended he wasn't there.

Seven

Sarah's Choice

When the girls were dressed and sat down for breakfast, Sarah said she would feed Luis when he woke up. That made Mrs. Mendez very happy. She was cooking at the stove, listening to music, and singing along with it.

The girls put syrup on their pancakes, but Mr. Mendez put beans on top of his pancake and rolled it up like a rug.

"He puts beans on everything!" said Mercedes. Her uncle made a funny face.

Mrs. Mendez poured the girls some chocolate, but she called it Spanish chocolate. It was very dark and thick.

Syrup

The baby woke up, and Mrs. Mendez ate her breakfast while Sarah fed Luis his strained bananas and cereal. Luis sneezed, and cereal went all over Sarah's shirt. She just laughed.

"I can always wash my shirt," she said.

"Sarah's going to tell her class about Mexico," said Mercedes. "She has to choose a country."

"Tell them that all the men in Mexico are good-looking," said Mr. Mendez.

"Tell them that the women have lovely voices and sing all day," Mrs. Mendez said.

"Could Sarah borrow one of my skirts to wear to school? And some of my bracelets?" Mercedes asked her aunt.

"Of course," said Mrs. Mendez. "Look around the apartment, Sarah, and see if there are other things you might want to show your class."

"Well, maybe a tablecloth," said Sarah, looking at the beautiful lace cloth with the flowers stitched on it.

Mercedes took out a Mexican straw basket. "I'll look for things you can take to school, Sarah. When it's time for you to talk to the class, you can carry it with you," she said.

"And take some books about Mexico, too," said Mercedes's aunt.

This was much better than being Queen of England, Sarah decided.

When Sarah was leaving to go home, Mercedes gave her one of her bracelets to wear when she went to school. It was red and blue and black.

"This one is for you to keep," Mercedes said.

Sarah politely said thank you. "It's beautiful," she said.

Sarah said thank you to Mercedes's uncle Carlos for letting her come. She said thank you to Mercedes's aunt Gloria for making such a good dinner. She even said thank you to Leon for playing alligator with them, although the woman below *did* tap on her ceiling with a broom handle.

And she *almost* said thank you to Luis for letting her feed him. When Sarah was polite, she was *very* polite.

She put all of her things in her bag. She walked politely out the door. She walked politely down the hall to the stairs. Then she ran all the way down to the third floor, all the way down to the second, and all the way down to the first.

With her bag bumping against her leg, she threw open the door to the street and ran to the building next door.

She rushed through the door of her own building. She had just started to run across the lobby when . . . *SPLAT!*

Mr. Gurdy was mopping the floor, and Sarah slipped on the soapy tiles. Down she went.

Mr. Gurdy turned around. He saw Sarah on the floor and helped her to her feet.

"Are you hurt?" he asked.

"I skinned my knee," she said.

"Do you always run through the lobby at ninety miles an hour?" asked Mr. Gurdy. "Take your time. The building's not going anywhere."

"I have a lot to tell about Mexico!" Sarah said. She rubbed her knee and ran upstairs. By the time she reached the loft, she had forgotten all about her fall.

Mom was drinking coffee. Riley was eating toast.

"Mexico!" Sarah yelled.

Mom jumped. Riley dropped his toast.

"Good heavens!" said Mom. "Are you home already?"

"Guess what?" Sarah said. "I got a bracelet from Mercedes. And I've chosen my country to share with the class. It's Mexico."

"That's even better than England," Mom said.

"I think so, too," said Sarah. She showed them the bracelet.

"It's lovely," said Mom. "But what about

the long dress I made for you? What about the crown?"

"I'll wear them on Halloween," said Sarah. "I'll be a beautiful queen."

"Perfect," said Mom. "So tell me about the sleepover."

"What did you have to eat?" Riley wanted to know.

"We ate enchiladas with eggs," Sarah said. "And they gave me some books to read about Mexico."

"Good! Then you can share them with us," said Mom.

That afternoon, when Riley was watching TV, there was a knock at the door. It was Mercedes. She was carrying the Mexican straw basket. Inside the basket Sarah saw:

A skirt with green and orange and yellow flowers on it for Sarah to wear to school.

A blouse with lace around the sleeves.

A sombrero, or hat.

A little donkey and cart made of straw.

Huaraches, or sandals.

Some Mexican pesos, or coins.

A tablecloth with lace around it.

A small Mexican flag, with a green stripe, a white stripe, and a red one.

A Mexican cookbook with pictures of Mexican foods.

And a beautiful picture frame made of tin.

"My father was a tinsmith," said Mercedes. "He made beautiful things out of tin. He made this for me."

These things were very special, Sarah knew. She could hardly wait to walk into the classroom wearing the Mexican clothes, with the bracelet on one arm and the basket on the other.

But when she looked at her friend, Mercedes looked sad. Sarah didn't know whether she was thinking about her parents and the earthquake or about how she could not speak Spanish at her school.

And suddenly Sarah, the Idea Girl, had another idea. A wonderful idea. A super idea!

"Mom," she said, "wouldn't it be fun if I could take *Mercedes* to school?"

"That would be *very* special," said Mom. "Would you like that, Mercedes?"

"Yes!" Mercedes said. "I could wear my Mexican clothes, too. We would be dressed like sisters."

Sarah clapped her hands. She grabbed Mercedes, and they danced around the floor.

Mom went to the telephone and called Mrs. Mendez.

Mercedes's aunt said she would send a note to Mercedes' school on Monday, asking if Mercedes could go to Sarah's school for one day.

"Let's keep it a secret," said Sarah. "Don't let anyone know, not even Peter."

Mercedes agreed.

Sarah looked around. Riley was still watching TV.

"Not *anyone*," said Sarah. "Especially Riley, because he'd tell!"

Eight

Yams and Legs and Chopsticks

At dinner that evening, Mom asked, "I wonder why Mercedes is living with her aunt and uncle. Has she ever told you, Sarah?"

"Yes," Sarah said. "Her parents were killed in an earthquake. They were in a hotel."

"Oh, that is so sad," said Mom.

Riley looked as though he were going to cry. He got up and put his arms around his mother. "Don't ever stay in a hotel," he said in a small voice.

Mom smiled a little. "Riley, an earthquake

is very unusual. Why, it is far more dangerous to ride in a car than to stay in a hotel."

"Don't ever ride in a car," said Riley.

Mom hugged him back. "Listen, Riley. There are a lot of things that could happen to us right here at home, but they usually don't. I could choke on my food!"

"Don't ever eat," said Riley.

This time, Mom laughed. "Most people live to be very old," she said. "I plan to live until I am very, *very* old."

"Good," said Riley.

Monday was Nigeria Day at school. Peter arrived in a poncho. It was called an *agbada* in Nigeria. It was blue. He had on blue sandals to match.

"I chose Nigeria because my great-great-great-great-grandfather came from that part of Africa," Peter said.

He told the class that there were many different languages spoken in Nigeria, not just one.

NIGERIA
LAGOS

"What do they eat in Nigeria?" asked a boy named Jonathan.

"Yams," said Peter.

"What are those?" asked Sarah.

"They taste like sweet potatoes," Peter said.

Then he told about making candy in Nigeria. He said that they boil sugar and water and honey and almonds together. Then they pull at it like taffy. And, just as Sarah feared, he passed around some Nigerian candy.

Sarah didn't have any candy to pass around. She wondered if the class would like Mexico Day.

"You did a fine job with Nigeria Day, Peter," said Mrs. Gold. "If your great-great-great-great-grandfather were still alive, he would be very proud of you."

The day after that was Italy Day. Italy was the country Emily had chosen. She said that she had been to Italy once. Her family had gone to Venice, where many of the streets were canals. They got around town on a boat instead of in a taxi.

"*Pinocchio* was written by an Italian," said Emily. Then she told an Italian story. It was called "Fearless John." It was about a boy who wasn't afraid of anything.

"He even spent the night in a haunted castle," said Emily. "A leg came down the chimney. Then another leg."

Everybody laughed.

"Then two arms and a head," said Emily.

The class laughed again.

"When all the pieces were down the chimney, they put themselves together and became a giant. But John wasn't afraid. Because John was so brave, the giant gave him lots of gold."

"Is that the end of the story?" asked Sarah.

"No. One sunny day, John was walking in his garden. He saw something big and black moving along the path in front of him," said Emily. "He was so scared, he died."

"What was it?" asked Peter.

"His shadow," said Emily. "The end."

Everyone clapped.

"You are doing very well, class, in telling us about other countries," said the teacher. "I can hardly wait to hear from the rest of you."

Sarah swallowed. Would Mexico Day be as good as Italy Day and Nigeria Day?

Thursday was China Day, and Tim Wong gave out chopsticks from his father's restaurant. He wore a Wongs' T-shirt with a big red dragon on the front that Sarah's mother had designed.

He had pictures of the Great Wall of China. He said it took hundreds of years to build it. He said it started out as a lot of short walls until it was one thousand five hundred miles long.

The bigger and longer the Wall of China became, the smaller and smaller Sarah felt. Peter had brought Nigerian candy for all the class. Emily had brought a funny story. Tim had brought chopsticks, and who knew what the others were going to bring. Sarah was going to talk about Mexico, but none of her relatives had ever lived there. Should she have been Queen of England after all?

"What are you going to do tomorrow for Mexico Day?" asked Peter as they walked home from school together. "What are you bringing to class?"

"It's a secret," said Sarah.

Nine

Mercedes' Day

When Sarah got out of bed the next morning, she brushed her teeth and her hair so fast that Mom made her do it again.

Then she put on the white Mexican blouse with lace around the sleeves that Mercedes had loaned her.

She put on the Mexican skirt with the green and orange and yellow flowers.

She tried on the sandals, but they were too big, so she put them back in the basket.

"I'm too excited to eat breakfast," she told her mother.

"You must eat breakfast," Mom said.

"No leaving this apartment until you've had your breakfast."

Sarah ate half a bowl of Rice Chex, and then she put on her coat, picked up her Mexican straw basket, and went down the stairs to apartment 303. She knocked on Peter's door.

"Who is this strange little girl who looks as though she came from Mexico?" asked Granny Belle.

Sarah grinned.

"You look very different," Peter told her when he came to the door.

"It's only the clothes," said Sarah, although she wished she had long black hair like Mercedes's.

They went down the stairs to the lobby. Mercedes was waiting for them by the door. She had on a Mexican dress. She was wearing beads around her neck and Mexican shoes on her feet.

"Why aren't you at your school?" Peter asked her.

"Because I'm going to your school today," said Mercedes. "I'm going for Mexico Day."

Peter was very surprised.

"Only *I'm* going to call it Mercedes Day!" Sarah said happily.

The two girls pretended they were sisters. They each took hold of the Mexican basket. They carried it between them all the way to school. Mercedes's shoes made squeaky sounds when she walked, and she laughed with each step.

Everyone was curious about the new girl.

"This is Mercedes Mendez," Sarah told them. "She was born in Mexico. She's here to help me talk about her country."

"Welcome to our class, Mercedes," said Mrs. Gold. She found a special place for Mercedes to sit.

Mrs. Gold let her read in Sarah's group when they got out their readers. She let her go first in line at lunch.

When it was time for the lesson about other countries, Sarah stood up in front of the room. She showed the class everything that was in the basket. She told them all she knew about Mexico.

Sarah said that the capital of Mexico was Mexico City and that the official language was Spanish. She said that there was a festival, or fiesta, every day of the year somewhere in Mexico. There was always a holiday to celebrate. Then Sarah told about the sleepover at Mercedes's apartment and what they had eaten for dinner and breakfast.

When Sarah was through, Mercedes stood up. She told how her parents were killed in an earthquake. The class was very quiet. But then she told how kind her uncle

Carlos and aunt Gloria had been to her, and the class looked happy again.

"You said you have only been in the United States about six months, Mercedes," the teacher said. "How did you learn to speak English so well?"

"In Mexico I learned a little English," Mercedes explained. "And here my aunt Gloria sends me to a special school where we can't speak Spanish at all. We can't wear Mexican clothes or sing Mexican songs. We have to learn to be Americans very fast, and *then* we can sing about Mexico." She smiled. "That's why I liked coming here today."

"We're very glad to have you," said Mrs. Gold. "Would you sing a Mexican song for us?"

Mercedes looked a little embarrassed. Then she said, "I'll sing it first in Spanish, and then I'll sing it in English."

It was a song called "Las Mañanitas." It was about waking up and hearing birds singing. The words sounded strange to Sarah, but then Mercedes sang it in English.

Sarah thought about how strange these English words would sound to the children in Mexico!

"You girls did very well," Mrs. Gold said when the class was over. "That was a wonderful idea to bring Mercedes to school, Sarah. Today was one of our best."

Sarah thought so, too.

As she walked home with Mercedes, the two girls held the straw basket between them. Sarah said, "I'm sorry about your

parents, but I'm glad that you're my friend."

"So am I!" Mercedes said. "Do you know how to say 'friend' in Spanish? It's *amigo* if it's a boy, or *amiga* if it's a girl."

"Then you're my *amiga*," said Sarah.

"And you're mine," Mercedes told her.